Hurry up!

Come join me.

Fish Eyes

A BOOK YOU CAN COUNT ON

Lois Ehlert

Harcourt Children's Books
Houghton Mifflin Harcourt
Boston   New York

Dedicated to Beaver Dam Lake—
those who live in it and those
who live around it.

Copyright © 1990 by Lois Ehlert

All rights reserved. For information about permission
to reproduce selections from this book, write to Permissions,
Houghton Mifflin Harcourt Publishing Company, 215 Park
Avenue South, New York, New York 10003.

Harcourt Children's Books is an imprint of Houghton Mifflin
Harcourt Publishing Company.

www.hmhbooks.com

The Libaray of Congress has cataloged the hardcover
edition as follows:
Fish Eyes: a book you can count on/by Lois Ehlert.
p. cm.
Summary: A counting book depicting the colorful fish
a child might see if he turned into a fish himself.
ISBN 0-15-228050-2
ISBN 0-15-228051-0 (pbk)
[1. Fish—Fiction.   2. Stories in rhyme.   3. Counting.]
1. Title
PZ8.3E29Fi   1990
[E]—dc20   89-15352

Manufactured in Malaysia
TWP 20
4500409648

What a tail!

If I could put on a suit of scales,

add some fins and one of these tails,

I'd close my eyes and then I'd wish

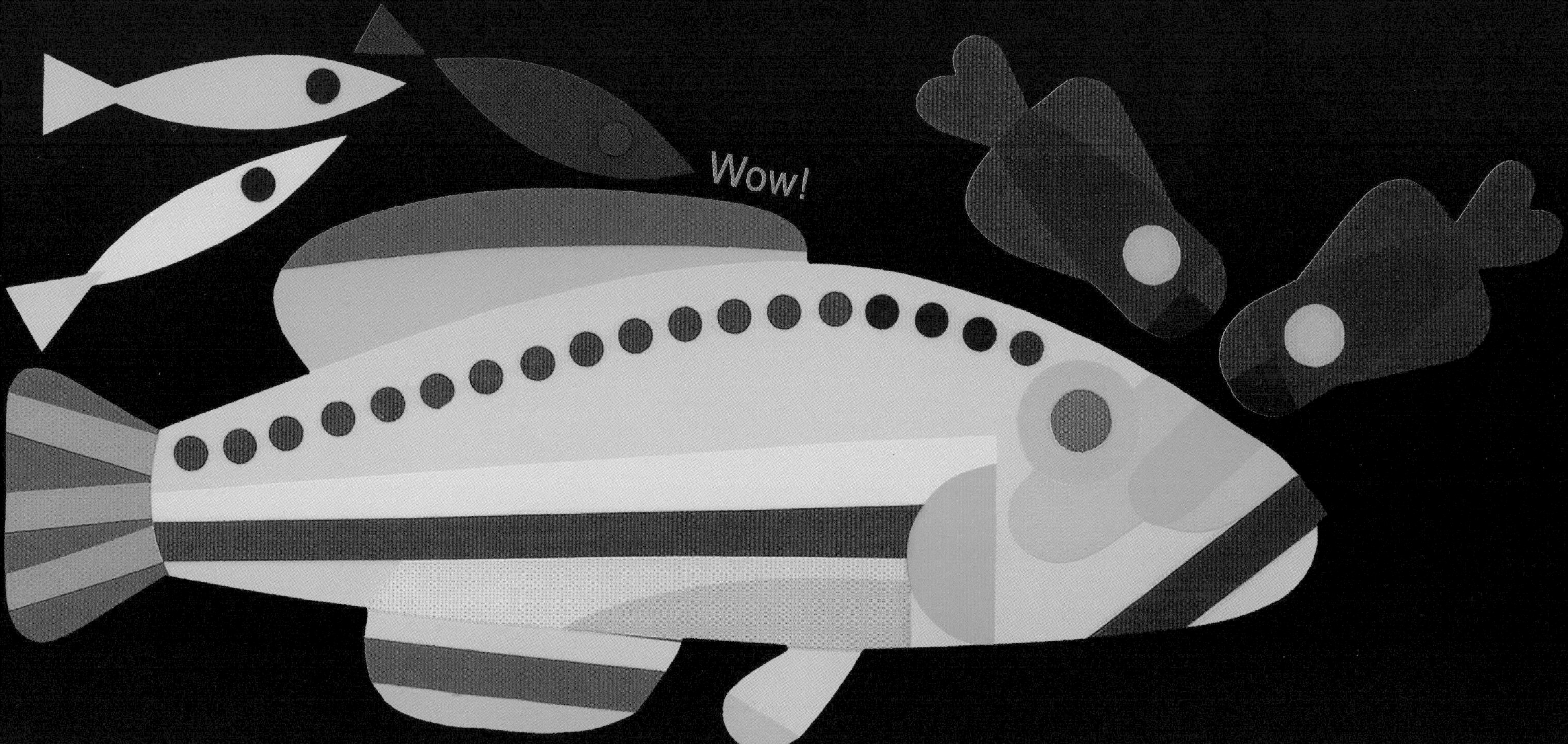

that I'd turn into a beautiful fish.

Will you dance with me?

I'd flip down rivers and splash in the sea.

I'd swim so far you would never catch me.

I'd see:

Follow me.

1 one green fish

1 green fish plus me makes 2

2 two jumping fish

2 jumping fish
plus me makes 3

3 three smiling fish

3 smiling fish
plus me makes 4

4 four striped fish

4 striped fish
plus me makes 5

5 five spotted fish

5 spotted fish
plus me makes 6

6 six fantailed fish

6 fantailed fish
plus me makes 7

7 seven flipping fish

7 flipping fish plus me makes 8

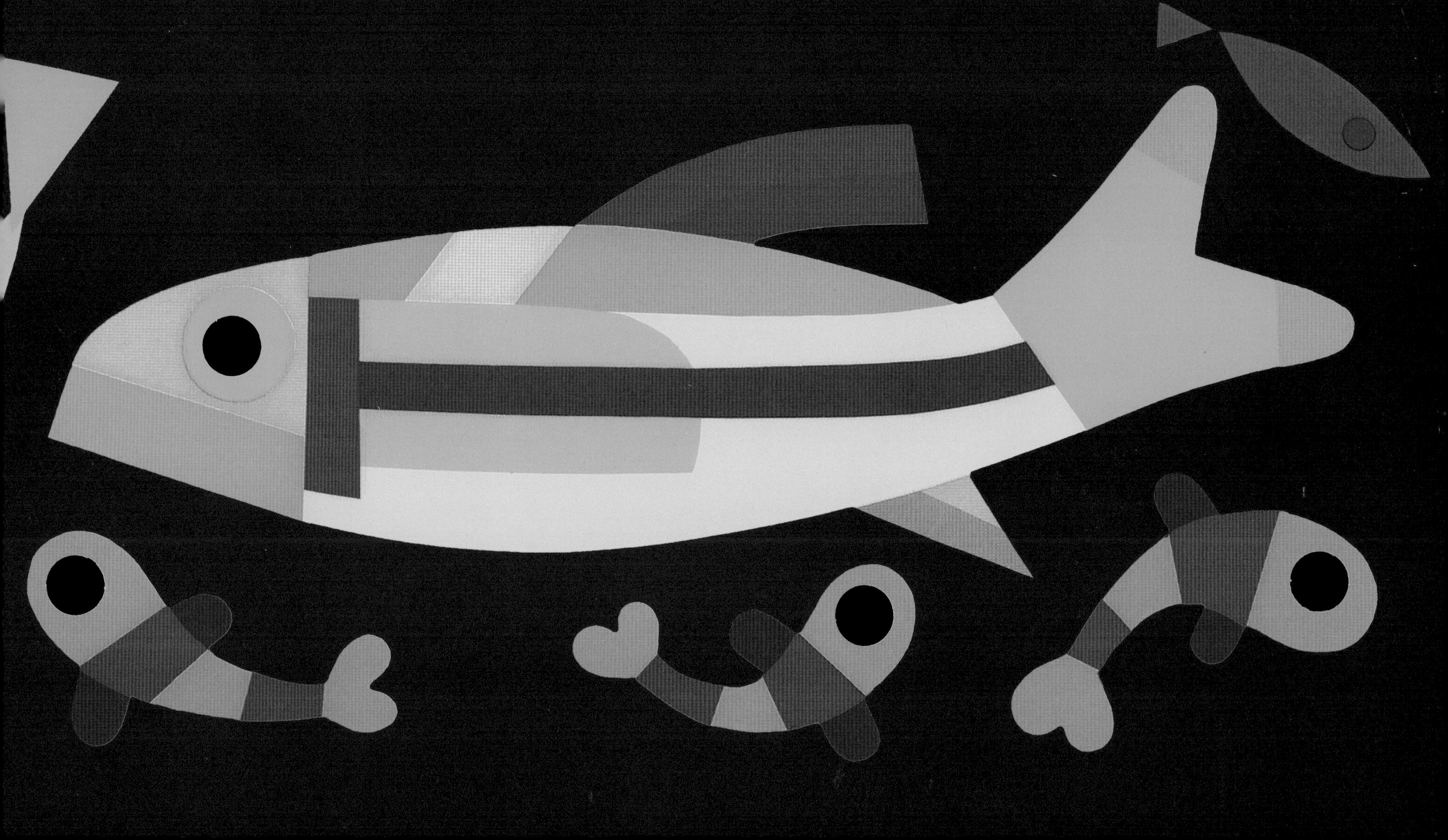

8 eight skinny fish

8 skinny fish
plus me makes 9

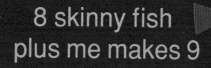

9 nine flashy fish

9 flashy fish plus me makes 10

10 ten darting fish

10 darting fish,
so long!

Keep flipping!

Then I'd keep swimming until I would see

all of those fish eyes looking at me.

If you could truly have a wish,
would you wish to be a fish?